For my mum, with much love—G. R.

First published by Macmillan Children's Books in 2003
First American Edition, 2003

For information address Hyperion Books for Children,
114 Fifth Avenue, New York, New York 10011-5690.

1 3 5 7 9 10 8 6 4 2

ISBN 0-7868-1925-1
Library of Congress Cataloging-in-Publication Data on file.

Printed in Belgium

Visit www.hyperionchildrensbooks.com

BRIAN & BOB

The Tale of Two Guinea Pigs

by Georgie Ripper

HYPERION BOOKS FOR CHILDREN · NEW YORK

Brian the guinea pig lived in a nice comfy cage in Pete's Pet Palace, with his best friend, Bob.

Brian had short, shiny fur of which he was very proud. Bob had long, tufty fur, which he didn't really think about all that much.

The two little guinea pigs spent their days doing
what guinea pigs do best—eating, sleeping, and
playing I Spy.

Brian was really good at I Spy, and almost always won with clever words like *parakeet gravel.*

One day, Brian and Bob were busy playing when a little boy walked into the shop.

"I spy with my little eye," Bob began—but before he could finish, the little boy reached into the cage and picked him up.

"I want this one," the boy said. "I'll call him Fluffy."

Brian watched as Bob was put into a cardboard box with holes in the lid. He just had time to wave good-bye before Bob was gone.

Suddenly the cage felt very big and empty.

Brian missed Bob already. So he trundled
off to find a peanut to cheer himself up.

But it didn't cheer
him up at all.

In fact, every day Brian missed Bob more and more,
and every day he felt more and more miserable.

Then, one day, Brian was sitting in his cage feeling sad, when he noticed an old man peering down at him.

The man picked him up and smiled. "He's just what I was looking for," he said, and he put Brian into a box.

At first Brian was excited. "Maybe there will be another guinea pig in my new home," he said to himself.

But that evening, he found himself all alone again. Brian wished he was back in Pete's Pet Palace. At least he could talk to the goldfish there.

"I wonder what's happened to Bob," whispered Brian. "He's probably forgotten all about me by now." He wiped away a tear and curled up in the straw.

The next morning, Brian hadn't even opened his eyes when he felt his box being lifted up.

"What's happening now?" he grumbled. But he didn't really care. Things couldn't get much worse than they already were.

He drifted back to sleep, dreaming of Pete's Pet Palace and of winning a peanut-throwing contest with Bob.

A little while later, Brian was awakened by a buzz of excited voices outside his box. He was annoyed.

"Can't I at least have some peace and quiet?"

Then, suddenly, the lid was lifted off, and bright light streamed into the box.

Brian looked up to see a
little boy smiling down at him.
Sleepily, he wondered if he had seen
the boy somewhere before.

The boy picked Brian up and gave him the biggest hug he'd ever had.

"Oh, thank you, Grandpa!" he said happily. "He's just what I wanted. I'm going to call him Snuffles."

The little boy put Brian into his new cage.

Brian stretched out and sniffed the air.

"That's funny," he said, and sniffed again.

As Brian watched, a pile of hay in the corner
started to move, and all of a sudden . . .

BRIAN

Brian was so excited to see Bob that he thought he would burst with happiness.

By that evening, sitting together in their cage playing I Spy, the two little guinea pigs had almost forgotten they had ever been apart. "I spy with my little eye," said Bob, "something beginning with—"

But Brian was already fast asleep.